Ada Lace

Gets Famous

Ada Lace

Gets Famous

• AN ADA LACE ADVENTURE •

EMILY CALANDRELLI

WITH TAMSON WESTON

ILLUSTRATED BY RENÉE KURILLA

Simon & Schuster Books for Young Readers

New York London Toronto Sydney New Delhi

For Rose and Lincoln: may your greatness be matched
only by your goodness.
—E. C.

For Milo.
—T. W.

For Dee (aka @sciencewithdee), a young scientist and
Ada fan who inspires me to always keep learning!
—R. K.

SIMON & SCHUSTER BOOKS FOR YOUNG READERS
An imprint of Simon & Schuster Children's Publishing Division
1230 Avenue of the Americas, New York, New York 10020
This book is a work of fiction. Any references to historical events, real people, or real places are used fictitiously. Other names, characters, places, and events are products of the author's imagination, and any resemblance to actual events or places or persons, living or dead, is entirely coincidental.
Text © 2023 by Emily Calandrelli
Cover illustration © 2023 by Renée Kurilla
Cover design by Laurent Linn © 2023 by Simon & Schuster, Inc.
Interior illustration © 2023 by Renée Kurilla
All rights reserved, including the right of reproduction in whole or in part in any form.
SIMON & SCHUSTER BOOKS FOR YOUNG READERS
and related marks are trademarks of Simon & Schuster, Inc.
For information about special discounts for bulk purchases, please contact Simon & Schuster Special Sales at 1-866-506-1949 or business@simonandschuster.com.
The Simon & Schuster Speakers Bureau can bring authors to your live event.
For more information or to book an event, contact the Simon & Schuster Speakers Bureau at 1-866-248-3049 or visit our website at www.simonspeakers.com.
Also available in a Simon & Schuster Books for Young Readers hardcover edition.
Interior design by Tom Daly
The text for this book was set in Minister Std.
The illustrations for this book were rendered digitally.
Manufactured in the United States of America
0623 OFF
First Simon & Schuster Books for Young Readers paperback edition October 2023
2 4 6 8 10 9 7 5 3 1
CIP data for this book is available from the Library of Congress.
ISBN 9781665931175 (hc)
ISBN 9781665931168 (pbk)
ISBN 9781665931182 (ebook)

Ada Lace

Gets Famous

Chapter One
FIRST-DAY BLUES

I see poor George got another makeover," said Mr. Lace. The robot zipped over into the corner.

"I prefer 'update,' Dad. Makeovers are for reality TV," said Ada.

"I'm tired," said George. He switched himself off.

"Well, as long as it keeps you from 'updating' my electric razor again, I'm fine with it—whatever you call it."

"Your razor is intact," said Ada. She bent over to examine George. He didn't seem to want to turn back on again.

Elliott had been watching *Bob the Robot* when Ada had gotten the idea for the latest update. She liked the look of Bob the Robot's head. Her

dad had a point—the change was cosmetic. But that wasn't the only reason for it. Ada and Tycho had recently gotten into taking things apart and putting them back together again—sometimes in ways the manufacturer hadn't intended.

"My car!" yelled Elliott from his room. "It won't go!"

Ada had been wondering when Elliott would discover that. She went into Elliott's room to find him aiming the remote control at the empty shell of the car. He was still pressing the button.

"Oh, it goes," said Ada. "It's just not exactly a car anymore." Ada took the remote from Elliott and aimed it at a pile of plush toys. A stuffed ladybug came scuttling out of the corner.

"Hahaha! Isn't that fun?" said Ada.

"No! A car is fun. I want my car!" said Elliott.

"I guess I'll just save my innovations for someone who appreciates them," said Ada. She got busy pulling the wheels and wires out of the ladybug.

Ada had not expected to enjoy the summer so much. Nina had gone to camp in Marin, and Milton and his family had gone to San Diego. Ada had two weeks of EggHead camp, but other than that, she thought she would be left to her own devices. That could be fun sometimes, but she was also prepared to be a little lonely.

To her surprise, though, Tycho ended up spending most weeks with his uncle, Mr. Peebles. So, all summer, Ada and Tycho took apart old calculators, electric toys, radios, computer monitors, and a lot of other stuff people threw out. Sometimes they made new things from them. Most of what they made wasn't that useful, but if it lit up and made fun noises, that was good enough for them. After a while, Ada found she couldn't stop. Every time she saw a device, she wanted to know what was inside. Sometimes it got her into trouble.

"ADA!!!" Uh-oh. Mr. Lace stormed into Elliott's bedroom. "Why is my electric bike in pieces?"

"Uh . . . I was just having a little peek. I'll get it back together. I just wanted to make sure it was, um, safe for you to use!"

"I want it together before school starts."

"No problem, Dad! Tycho is coming this weekend and I'm going to get Mr. Peebles to help. . . ."

"School starts tomorrow, Ada," said Mr. Lace.

"Oh, wow. Right. Time really flies, huh? Heh."

Mr. Lace was not amused.

The first day of school did not go well. Ada had stayed up late trying to get the bike together and overslept—like, seriously overslept. George still wasn't turning on, apparently, so he didn't wake her up. She almost wore her pj top to school. Ms. Lace was disappointed that they couldn't manage the usual first-day photo.

"I guess we'll have to do it the second day," she said.

Ada didn't even have time to sit down and eat pancakes. Her dad rolled one up and wrapped it in a napkin so she could eat it on the way to school. As they were leaving, suddenly George beeped to life.

"Time for dinner!" he said.

"Thanks, George," said Ada as she flew out the door.

Since Ada was running late, Nina met her in front of the school.

"Your shirt's on backward," she said.

"Aw, crud," said Ada.

"Maybe it's the style? It could be the style," Nina said.

Ada breezed past her to the restroom as

quickly as she could and turned the shirt around in one of the stalls. She was three minutes late for class.

The rest of the day wasn't much better. She had to share Nina's lunch because she had left hers on the counter. She didn't have her favorite notebook, or a pencil, so she had to borrow those, too. Mr. Lace had a meeting after school, so Ada and Nina would be walking home with Crystal, a high-school girl who watched them sometimes.

"Just be sure to pay attention to your phone," said Mr. Lace. "We gave it to you so I could reach you, not just so you could play chess and watch videos."

"Geez, Dad. Okay," said Ada.

"I'm sorry, sweetie. It's a stressful time of year," said Mr. Lace.

Ada knew that, but this year seemed

particularly stressful for Mr. Lace. Ada met Nina and Crystal in front of the school.

Nina looked over a photocopied sheet of paper from school.

"Gosh, the school supply list is long, huh?" said Nina.

"Ugh," said Ada. "I left mine in my desk—with all the other first-day forms. This day is the worst."

"I'm sure your dad will have it. Plus, it's online," said Nina.

"Lucky you can get it online," said Crystal.

"What do you mean?" said Nina. "The internet is everywhere!"

"Not always. For one thing, you have to pay for it. And then you would need a computer or phone or some way to access it. Not everyone has that."

Ada had been complaining about forgetting papers, but she couldn't imagine what she would do without the internet. It made so many things easier. Suddenly she felt really fortunate, and a little bit guilty for complaining.

By the time Mr. Lace got home, Ada had the table cleared and set. It was already a quarter to six. She got right to work rinsing greens for the salad while her dad made sauce and started boiling water for pasta.

When they sat together at the dinner table, though, Mr. Lace seemed tired. Ada could tell that he was still upset about the bike, but she almost wished he would yell. It felt worse to have him be so quiet.

"Ada, you've gotta take a break from breaking things," Mr. Lace said. "School's started. We both have things to focus on. . . ."

"I'm not breaking things, I'm—"

"If I can't use it, it might as well be broken," said Mr. Lace. "And that bike costs a lot of money. I can't replace it if it's ruined."

"It's not, Dad. Tycho and I can fix it," said Ada. "I'm sorry."

Mr. Lace sighed and patted her hand.

They ate quietly for a few moments until Ada noticed a piece of paper on the table. It was the school supply list Mr. Lace had brought home.

"Paper towels . . . hand sanitizer . . . tissues . . . Why do we have to buy all this stuff anyway? Why doesn't the school pay for it?"

"Well, the school doesn't have money for

everything. So, we have to . . . fill in the gaps. And there happen to be a lot of gaps this year."

"What did you have to buy when you were in school? Inkwells? Slates? Oats for the horse pulling the bus?"

Mr. Lace laid his fork down and raised an eyebrow at Ada.

"Are you actually asking me a question? Or just roasting me?"

"Aww, I was kidding, Dad!" said Ada. "I didn't mean it! You know you're the coolest art teacher I know."

He gave her a crooked smile as he poked at his rotini with his fork.

"Really, though, did your parents have to buy school supplies for you?"

"We had to buy notebooks and pencils, but the school provided a lot of the other stuff."

"Really? Well, why not now?"

"School is a bit different now. You kids need a lot more materials than we did, and with budget cuts every year, we simply don't get enough funds anymore. But we're actually relatively lucky. There are other schools worse off than ours and with a lot more students who have less than we do."

Ada was reminded of what Crystal had said earlier. She thought of all the kids, classrooms, and teachers who needed supplies but could only rely on themselves to get it. It wasn't fair.

Later that night Ada talked to Tycho on Speak-A-Boo, a video chat platform for people under thirteen. They talked about their first day and how topsy-turvy Ada's had been.

"I always feel a little messed up on my first

day—like I have to transition from being home Tycho to school Tycho."

"That's the thing—usually I don't mind the first day. At least until now," said Ada. "And on top of everything there's a huge list of supplies this year."

"Yeah, for us, too," said Tycho.

"It seems weird to me that the school doesn't just provide a lot of this stuff. And Dad says that some schools have even less than ours."

"I bet. Your neighborhood is pretty fancy, Ada."

"There must be a way to help," said Ada.

"Oh, definitely," said Tycho. "There's always a way to help."

"I suppose you're right," said Ada. She just had to think about how. At the moment, she felt a little overwhelmed.

"Speaking of help," said Ada. She gave Tycho a sheepish look. "I'm going to need your help to fix my dad's bike."

"Oh, he found it, huh?"

"Yep."

Chapter Two
The Public Awaits?

The next two days were a little better, but Ada was still looking forward to the weekend. Her mom said she must still have summer brain. All she could think about was the old laptop that Mr. Peebles had picked up for her and Tycho to mess around with. It wasn't working right and he seemed to think they might be able to figure out how to fix it. First they had to fix Mr. Lace's bike, though.

Ada wheeled it over on Saturday morning. Tycho was already waiting in front of his uncle's open garage with a tool kit. Ada set the bike on the workstand and Tycho wheeled in close for a better look.

"So, what's up?" said Tycho.

"For some reason, it makes a weird rattling noise when my dad uses it. I took the motor apart and tried to put it back together, but I think I made it worse. The rattling sound got even louder," Ada said.

Tycho leaned in for a closer look. "How old is this bike?" He opened the motor on the back wheel. "On e-bikes, the motor is what kicks on and helps make pedaling easier, but"—he paused as he inspected the motor more closely—"this one looks pretty old. The gears are all worn down."

"Yeah, my dad got it used. Must have been well-loved in its past life," Ada joked.

"Heh, looks like it. Here, we just need some new gears, maybe a few new bearings and some grease, and it'll be good as new."

"Do we have that stuff handy?" Ada looked around Mr. Peebles's garage.

Tycho wheeled over to a large cabinet and opened a drawer filled with gears. "I'm surprised you have to ask," he said with a smirk.

It took another forty-five minutes or so to get everything put back together and cleaned up. Mr. Lace brought over a pizza for lunch. They ate together in the garden. Mr. Lace asked the usual grown-up questions about school and how Tycho's mom was doing. Tycho started giving shorter and shorter answers until Mr. Lace wiped his hands on his napkin, stood up, and grabbed his bike by the handlebars.

"Good as new?" Mr. Lace asked.

"Even better!" Ada jumped up excitedly.

"Um, you might want to take it for a test

drive before we make that call," said Tycho.

Mr. Lace zipped off through the courtyard and out onto Polymer Street. The motor was whisper-quiet.

"That oughta keep him busy for a while," said Ada.

"All right," said Tycho. "Now let's check out this laptop." He rubbed his hands together and rolled over to a box on the stoop. He leaned over and pulled the box into his lap.

"This is a pretty new machine, but you know how things are in this town. Everyone wants the latest model. It's well-loved too, but it has a lot of promise."

Ada and Tycho thought that keeping a visual record would save them from winding up in the same situation she had run into with her dad's bike. If they got stuck while putting it back together, they could go back and see where every piece came from and what was missing. Ada attached her phone to the bike workstand with some elastic bands, just above where they were working. She opened the camera app and started

recording video. It was going to be a big project, and they weren't sure they'd finish the whole thing in one day. Once they had everything apart, Ada turned the phone on Tycho.

"Smile! I'm going to post this to SeeMe," she said. Ada had started following different creators on the kids-only video platform SeeMe. She loved watching kids do science experiment videos on there and even thought it might be fun to post her own videos there one day.

"Uh"—Tycho ducked away from the camera— "I'm a little camera-shy. And I'm pretty sure my mom wouldn't like it."

"Oh, sorry! I should have asked first." Ada pointed the phone back to the computer.

"But you should totally do it, Ada. It's probably way more interesting than a lot of the stuff that's on there now. You might be able to make some money, too."

"Huh," said Ada. "Maybe that's how we can help teachers get the supplies they need . . . I bet if we could raise ten thousand dollars, that would cover all the school supplies the teachers need at my school. . . ." Mr. and Ms. Lace *had* approved her posting videos on there, as long as they could see them first.

"Oh, right . . . ," said Tycho. "Yeah. That's an idea."

"So you'll do it with me?" said Ada.

"I could help behind the scenes," said Tycho. "But I don't know if I'll be here enough."

"Well, you're going to help with this video," said Ada.

"Hm, okay. Hand me that phone." He turned it around on Ada and prompted her, "Tell us what we're looking at, Ada."

They spent the rest of the day trying to reassemble the computer, but they didn't get as far as they had hoped. When Tycho's mom came to pick him up, it was already six o'clock and Ada had to go home for dinner.

Ada wanted to have a complete project to record, so she decided to start with something a little simpler than the computer. She borrowed her dad's desk lamp and a bendable snake toy from Elliott's room to hold her phone in place above her desk. Then she got to work on an old hair dryer. It took only half an hour to take it apart but another hour to put it together. Ada showed off the heating element and made sure to get some close-ups of the Nichrome wire that was responsible for making the air hot. She had to try a few times before it worked. Finally, Ada flicked the switch and a burst of hot air blasted in her face. A few minutes later the hair dryer stopped turning on again. Luckily, she'd already gotten what she needed for the video.

With the help of the internet and the software that came with her computer, she started editing her video. It was harder than she expected. For

one thing, she had ten times as much footage as she needed. Five minutes was supposed to be the ideal length for SeeMe. No one needed to watch every turn of every screw, so she sped that part up and cut some out. She wanted to make sure that viewers knew what was going on, so she added voice-over. Ada went into the nitty-gritty of Nichrome wire and explained how it's the same wire that's used in the toaster in your kitchen! She still had about two minutes left to cut when her mom came into her room just after ten.

"Ada. Bed!"

"But I'm almost done!" said Ada.

"That's what you said at nine thirty. And at nine forty-five," said Ms. Lace.

"Okay . . ."

Ada turned off her desk lamp and climbed

into bed. Ms. Lace pulled Ada's comforter up to her chin and gave her a kiss on the forehead. She turned off the overhead light and walked through the door. Then she turned back.

"Oh, Ada. You haven't seen my hair dryer, have you?" she asked.

"Uh . . ."

Ada fussed with the video for most of Sunday morning, cutting out a few seconds here, changing the audio there. She'd gotten down to five minutes, which was good. All the footage was of the hair dryer and her hands. Her hands were still dirty from working on the bike earlier. Hopefully, no one would notice. Sometimes her fingers got in the way of parts of the hair dryer, but she didn't have time to redo it. Ada wondered if she should just scrap the whole thing. But then she remembered what her dad always said—"Don't let perfection prevent completion!"—and decided that what she had was good enough.

SeeMe paid creators based on the number of views they got per video. Ada didn't have high hopes for making a ton of money, but she had heard of friends who had videos go viral with a few million views and made a couple thousand bucks. So just in case the impossible happened, Ms. Lace helped Ada with the financial side and connected her account to the family's bank account.

Ada hovered her mouse over the "publish" button on her SeeMe account, and after a long moment of hesitation, she whispered, "Here goes nothing," and pressed down on the mouse pad.

• • •

By Wednesday the video only had twenty views, which was precisely the same number of people she had emailed the video to and asked to watch it. Clearly, she was not meant for SeeMe stardom.

She checked the numbers again when she woke up Thursday morning and once more after breakfast. She didn't know what she was expecting.

"Something wrong?" Nina asked her on the way to school.

"My video is tanking," said Ada.

"It's just the first one, though," said Nina. "They'll get better."

"You've watched it, right?"

"Of course," said Nina.

"So? What did you think?" asked Ada.

Nina started fiddling with her hair. She always did that when she was afraid to tell the truth.

"I was a little distracted. I don't know if I could really say what was working and what wasn't."

"Come on, Nina," said Ada.

"Well, it didn't feel very . . . sticky."

"Sticky . . . What do you mean?" Ada looked skeptical.

"You need to make your audience feel hooked, like their eyes are stuck on your video and they can't stop watching! I think you could do that with more . . . artful storytelling."

"Well, I told everything I possibly could about how hair dryers work—the fan, the heating element . . . I even dove into the material science of Nichrome wire!"

"You may have dived a little too deep into Nichrome wire. . . . ," Nina said softly as she looked away.

"What was that?"

"Nothing, nothing. Ada . . . if you want to get a lot of views, you're going to need more art with your science."

"And help," said Ada. "I need help."

"Well, I can give you that," said Nina.

Ada spent that afternoon at Nina's. Nina had recently set up a space in her room she called "Creation Corner," which turned out to be great for shooting video. It was across from the windows, so there was some natural light. Nina used it to Speak-A-Boo with her aunt and her cousins. She also had a decent camera she had bought herself to photograph her artwork for her website.

"I've actually started to shoot a few room-decorating videos myself," said Nina. "But they're not quite ready yet."

Nina had an old clamp light from Mr. Peebles's

workshop clipped to a broomstick she'd stuck in a bucket filled with gravel. A desk lamp was propped on a stepladder on the opposite side. Nina had made a third light with some sticky strings of LEDs and a cake pan. It was wrapped in a T-shirt to diffuse the light and positioned near the floor. Nina moved the three different lights around until they surrounded the chair in Creation Corner.

Nina closed one eye, made L shapes with her fingers, and put her hands together to frame the shot.

"Now, this is art! The first thing you needed was better lighting. It was hard to see some of the stuff you mentioned in your voice-over. And the desk light you have made your skin look a little weird."

Ada had never thought about how her skin looked on camera before. But Nina was the one

with the artistic eye, so Ada trusted her.

"Mr. Peebles's clamp light is what they call the key light," Nina explained. "My little cake pan light is the fill light. It makes it so my face doesn't look too shadowy and scary."

"But we're not showing faces, right?" said Ada.

"I was going to mention that, Ada," said Nina. "On SeeMe they want to see YOU! It'll help your audience connect with you."

Nina pointed to her chair. She adjusted the camera. Ada sat down. She suddenly felt really self-conscious. Filming her hands was one thing, but with all those lights and the big camera looking right at her? It was ten times worse.

"Maybe I should wear a Halloween mask? Or use puppets?" said Ada. "Or maybe you could sit here instead!'

"Don't be silly!" said Nina. "This is your project. And you look great! Smile!"

Ada showed her teeth but her eyes looked terrified.

"Uh, maybe smile on the inside," said Nina.

Ada closed her eyes and imagined a smile.

"What are you doing?" Nina asked.

"I'm smiling on the inside!" said Ada.

"Okay, but at some point, perhaps the smile could also make its way to your face."

This time Ada bent her mouth into a U shape.

"You look like you're swallowing something gross," said Nina. "What can I do to make this easier for you?"

"Maybe you could point the camera somewhere else?"

"Ada . . ."

Ada put her fingers in the corners of her mouth and pulled. She stuck her tongue out and crossed her eyes. Nina lifted her face from the camera and pushed her nose up like a pig's. Ada laughed.

"Perfect!" said Nina. "Now I just need to make pig faces at you for a few hours."

Nina showed her the little clip she had just made. Ada laughed.

"That's not bad!" said Ada. "Who knew it would be so easy."

"It'll get easier when you forget the camera is there," said Nina.

"You're right. The lighting is really nice," said Ada. "I only have my desk lamp at home."

"Why don't you just shoot here? I mean, I have everything," said Nina.

"You don't mind? What about your videos?" asked Ada. "Don't you want to get your own channel started?"

"It'll be more fun to work on something together," said Nina. "Maybe you can help me with mine later."

"You're the best!"

Crystal picked Ada up from Nina's to walk her home. Crystal had her cousin Tanya with her. Tanya was around the same age as Elliott and they were instant friends. On the first day they met, it took Crystal and Tanya fifteen minutes longer than usual to get back home because Elliott and Tanya insisted on leapfrogging all the way across Juniper Garden before parting ways.

When Ada, Crystal, and Tanya arrived at the Lace household, Elliott was so excited to see Tanya and told her that he had a million things to show her. He ran through the whole list in the first fifteen seconds.

"Tanya, check out my remote control car. It's cool, right? And I have this bug robot. Maybe they can race? Or we could play Mario Kart. I wish we could play with my Tamagotchi— y'know, those digital pets? But it got ruined in the sand pit at school like all my friends' Tamagotchis."

Ada could hear Elliott running all around his room, from corner to corner. She imagined his floor covered in all his favorite stuff.

". . . Or we could just play this game if you want?"

Ada heard the familiar rattle of Connect 4 pieces.

"I'm really good at it. I also have a glow-in-the-dark soccer ball. It has a disco mode, too! Check it out. Wait, why do you want to play with that? That's not really that cool. That's just my dad's old tablet."

Ada was curious, so she went in to peek. Mr. Lace had given Elliott his tablet when he upgraded, but Elliott was never interested in it. He used it for schoolwork sometimes, but that was it.

"I just need to check something." Tanya was sitting in Elliott's beanbag chair on the floor, looking intently at the tablet.

"Don't you want to play with Elliott?" Ada asked.

"Oh, yeah! But I just have to do this one thing first," said Tanya. "I was trying to use the computers at the library, but the line was too long and Crystal had to pick me up before it was my turn. I need to finish this assignment or I'll get a zero."

Ada remembered what Crystal had said about not everyone having a way to get on the internet.

"You don't have a tablet to use at home," Ada said.

Tanya looked a little embarrassed.

"You can have that one if you want it," said Elliott.

"What? No, it's too expensive," said Tanya.

"I can borrow my dad's for homework. He won't mind," said Elliott.

"But won't you get in trouble?" Tanya looked at Elliott, then over at Ada.

"No," said Ada. "I'm sure Dad will be okay with it."

"Then you can do your homework *later* and play *now!*" said Elliott.

Tanya still looked uncertain.

"It's okay," said Ada. "Take it. I think Elliott wants you to play with him."

Tanya put the tablet in her backpack. She grabbed a video game controller.

"I'm Bowser," she said.

"Wait, really? I'm always Bowser," said Elliott. "Don't you want to be Princess Peach?"

"Bowser," said Tanya. "I called it."

"Ugh. Fine."

Chapter Three
THAT OLD MILTON MAGIC

Nina's advice helped. Ada actually got used to sitting in front of the camera. For her second video, Ada wanted to do a "teardown" of an old hand mixer. (This time she asked for permission.) She would start by showing the hand mixer intact, then take it apart piece by piece before assembling it again. Unlike in the

first video, Ada would talk to the camera and explain what she was doing to her "audience."

Nina helped her shoot on Saturday afternoon, and they edited the footage on Sunday. Ada learned a lot from Nina. She could see how watching a person explain things on camera was more fun than just watching a set of hands move things around. This one could catapult her channel into the SeeMe stratosphere! Or at least earn a few dollars in her SeeMe account that Ada could put toward school supplies. She posted it on a Wednesday night. By Thursday she had twenty-five views.

"Don't worry, Ada, Mercury is in retrograde. It's not our fault that it didn't do well," Nina said.

"Nina, the movement of planets doesn't have any effect on—"

"We just need to fine-tune our art!" Nina said excitedly.

"Heh." Ada let the Mercury comment pass. "And maybe our science, too."

That meant more videos. They posted two more in the next two weeks—one was a teardown of a TV remote, and the other was an inside look at a toy piano. Ada was getting better at talking to the camera and keeping her technical explanations a bit shorter. The remote got one hundred views, and the toy piano got a thousand. Ada was excited, but she checked her SeeMe account and the videos had only raked in a few bucks. That could maybe cover a pencil pack?

The day after she posted her fourth video, Nina, Ada, and Milton were eating lunch together at school.

"I watched your last video, Ada," said Milton.

"Yeah?"

"Well, I watched half of it. Then I got bored," said Milton.

"Great. Thanks," said Ada.

"I thought I would be more interested in the inside of a toy piano than I was in a hand mixer, but it turns out the inside of a piano isn't that cool either," said Milton. "What I really want to see you fix is a Tamagotchi—the sand pit at school destroyed mine."

"You killed your digital pet?" said Nina. "That's it! I'm contacting animal services!"

"I'm not the only one! It looks like the whole school killed their Tamagotchi pets with sand. The buttons just don't work anymore."

"I can help you fix it," said Ada.

"Oh yeah? Thanks, Ada! I'll bring it over. Maybe you can help me fix my blackjack game, too. And my earbuds . . ."

"Wow," said Ada. "You really know how to break stuff, huh?"

"Nobody's better at it!" said Milton.

"Hmm . . . That gives me an idea!" said Nina.

• • •

That afternoon Ada and Milton stepped into Nina's "studio." They had to move things around for their new idea. Milton needed room to move. He also brought a bag full of broken stuff. There was a remote control car, a drone, another drone, a solar powered radio, an old watch he had gotten for Christmas when he was five, the Tamagotchi, and the blackjack game.

"Wow," said Ada. "You really do know how to break stuff."

"Told ya," said Milton.

"Where do we start?" asked Nina.

"Let's bring the Tamagotchi back from the dead," said Ada.

"Agreed," said Nina. "Poor thing."

The concept was simple. Milton would break the Tamagotchi, then Ada would come to the rescue. Ada didn't know why she had not just included Milton from the start. He was such a ham. He walked into the room, tripped over something off camera, and fell on his Tamagotchi. He looked at the Tamagotchi for a moment, then into the camera. After a moment he cried miserably, "Oh no! I broke it!"

Of course, Milton didn't actually cry. If he did, it probably wouldn't be so funny. Or would it? It was hard to tell what people liked in these videos.

The next section showed Ada sitting at a worktable. She looked at the Tamagotchi and said, "Don't worry. I'll fix it!" The rest of the video showed Ada fixing the Tamagotchi. She just had to open it and clean out the sand from under the buttons. She talked through the steps one by one so that people watching could see what the Tamagotchi looked like inside and maybe fix their own at home. Ada and her friends called the new series *Oh No! I Broke It!*

They finished editing the video the next afternoon. Then they posted it.

"Hey," said Milton. "You really fixed it."

"I told you," said Ada.

"Now we just wait for the views to roll in!" said Milton.

"Uh, it may take a while," said Ada. "I mean, it's been weeks and I still only have—"

"But now you have the old Milton magic on your side, Ada," said Milton. He patted her on the head.

"Yeah, okay," said Ada.

Chapter Four

SeeMe Stardom

The next day, Ada was heading to their usual table to join Nina and Milton at lunch. She hadn't checked her SeeMe account because she was sure the video had flopped like her other ones and she was too nervous to see the results. But just as she was sitting down, a few kids ran up to their table.

"Milton! Your video is so funny!"

"Oh my gosh, I'm still laughing!"

Ada looked at Nina, confused.

"Isn't it amazing?" Nina said.

Ada pulled out her phone to check the video: over a hundred thousand views. A wave of equal parts panic and excitement overcame her as she locked eyes with Nina.

"Are we . . . famous?" Ada whispered excitedly.

The next week they made an *Oh No! I Broke It!* about a remote control car. It was a perfect device for Milton's slapstick skills. Milton walked on camera and stepped on the car. His foot flew out from under him and he landed on his butt.

He stood, rubbing his butt and looking sadly into the camera. Then he said: "Oh no! I broke it."

Nina stopped filming so she could laugh. "Oh, Milton."

"Ouch," he said. "That actually hurt."

"The sacrifices we make for our art . . . ," said Nina.

Ada was nervous. She had to come after Milton. That meant she should up the stakes— snag the viewer. While Nina was busy setting up for Ada's part of the video, Ada looked in Nina's closet for some props, a funny costume, anything that would keep the laughs going. She found a bag of pom-poms Nina used for crafts and snuck off to the bathroom.

"I'll be right back!" she said.

Ada taped one big pom-pom to her nose and one to each shoe. Then she put her hair in pigtails

and added pom-poms to the top of the pigtails. She looked like this clown she used to watch on TV when she was little. The clown made her laugh sometimes. Maybe she could be the funny one too.

"Ada!! Are you done in there?" Milton called impatiently.

"I'm ready! Start shooting, Nina," said Ada.

She opened the door and cartwheeled through it. Then she turned toward the camera with one finger up and said, "I'll fiddle-dee-dee fix it!"

Nina turned the camera off. She looked confused.

"What was that?" asked Milton.

"I was trying something new," said Ada. "What do you think?"

"Uh, Ada," said Nina, "the video did well last

time. And since Milton is covering the comedy, maybe you can stick to the technical stuff? You know, just be yourself!"

"Yeah, okay," said Ada. She pulled off the pom-poms and sat down at the worktable. Ada felt even more self-conscious than before but did her best to sit up straight and smile. Nina called, "Action!" Ada hoped the smile showed on the outside, because she wasn't really feeling it on the inside.

The week after the car video, they did one about a toy drone. Views and subscribers increased with each video. The toy drone video got them up to a hundred thousand subscribers.

"Ugh! That's it?" said Milton. It was two days after they had posted the drone video.

"What do you mean?" said Ada. "This is our

most popular video. We've raised five thousand dollars for school supplies since we posted it. We're halfway toward our goal!"

"The *Smash It Up!* SeeMe dude has a million subscribers. And that guy . . . well, he's just not that funny," said Milton.

"Don't worry, Milton. This is a very good start," said Nina.

A good start? Ada suddenly felt like she was on a different planet.

Milton was a celebrity at school now. Every kid he passed in the hallway shouted, "Oh no! It's Milton!" Even teachers got in on the action. During music class Mr. Pendergrass handed out recorders. When he gave Milton one, he said, "Here you go, Milton. Don't break it!" All the kids started laughing.

• • •

Johnny Samuels, one of the most popular kids at school, invited Milton to his birthday. He was having something called a Smashbox Derby. Milton was supposed to be the emcee. Ada wouldn't have minded so much that she wasn't invited, but Milton wanted to reschedule their next shooting date.

"Can you believe the nerve?" Ada said to Nina on the way home from school.

"Well, actually, Ada, Johnny wants me to go too. You know, so I can shoot it," said Nina.

"That's great, Nina," said Ada, "but when are we going to shoot *our* next video?"

"How about Monday after school?" said Nina.

"But Saturday is our usual shooting date!" said Ada. "Remember? So we can have time to edit?"

"It's just this once. We can figure it out. Do

you have something else to do on Monday?" asked Nina.

Ada didn't, so she agreed to wait, but she was starting to feel like a third wheel.

On Monday Milton was in top form. He had borrowed an old checkered sport coat from his dad and a bowler hat from his uncle Earl.

"What's with the outfit?" asked Ada.

"It's good for laughs," said Milton.

"Can't argue with that," said Nina.

Nina set the camera up across from the chair that Milton was preparing to fall from.

"Now, Ada, when you come in, I'm thinking we should streamline things a bit," said Nina. She was behaving more and more like a director.

"Streamline?" Ada asked.

"Well, you know, simplify. Maybe you don't

have to go into quite as much detail about all the doodads, you know, so people, um, stay interested."

"What do you mean?" said Ada.

"Well, just don't explain as much about it," said Nina. "In fact, maybe you can just do most of the fixing off camera and then we can have you kind of do a quicker version on camera. Then you can just pop in, put a few things together, and say, 'I fixed it!'"

"Uh . . . okay," said Ada. "But when we started this, I—"

"That's a great idea," said Milton.

"Great, let's do it," said Nina.

The shooting went a lot quicker when Ada didn't have to actually fix anything or say too much about the doodads. In fact, they got the whole thing done in an hour. Ada asked Nina if she wanted her to stay for the edit.

"Uh, only if you want to," said Nina. "I've pretty much got it, though."

That left Ada to do homework and brood by herself.

A week later they shot their eighth video. They had "streamlined" the process so much that Ada hardly had to spend any time at all at Nina's. After two months and eight videos, *Oh No! I Broke It!* was as successful as Ada had hoped it would be. More so. They were able to raise ten thousand dollars, which covered all the school supplies the teachers needed. This was the goal. So why wasn't Ada happier?

She walked across Juniper Garden into her house, making her way through the living room and stepping over her dad, who was playing race cars with Elliott. Without looking up he said, "You're home earlier than I expected!"

"Yeah," Ada said. She went straight to her room and collapsed on her bed.

Mr. Lace knocked on her open door and stood tentatively in the doorway.

"What happened? Did you run into problems?" he asked.

"No," said Ada.

"Oh. Because it seems like it's all gravy from here. Everyone's impressed with how much money you made," Mr. Lace said.

"Great," said Ada. "That makes me happy."

"Yeah," said Mr. Lace, "you sound thrilled."

"I'm sorry," said Ada.

"Are you not having fun anymore?" asked Mr. Lace, as he walked into Ada's room and sat on the edge of her bed.

"No, actually," said Ada. "I'm not. I feel like Milton's the star and I'm just an extra—in my own show!"

"Is that why you started making these

videos?" Mr. Lace asked. "To become a star?"

Ada thought for a moment. "I guess not."

"We are all grateful, Ada. You and your friends have helped a lot. Just remember, you can quit doing this as soon as it stops being fun. You achieved your goal. Maybe now it's time for you to think about what you'd like to do next." He stood up and walked out of the room.

Milton got recognized everywhere but Ada got recognized once too, when she was at the library looking through old articles for her social studies project.

"Psssst . . . Do I know you from somewhere?" the girl asked.

Ada was about to explain, but the girl interrupted her. "Ya! You're that girl in Milton's videos, aren't you?"

On the Friday before they were supposed to shoot their next video, Ada rewatched their most recent one. Views were beginning to level off. Ada wasn't that concerned at first, but Milton and Nina seemed to be, so she thought she could analyze the video and brainstorm some ideas for what they could work on. The video wasn't that different from the ones that came before it. Milton fell backward through the door, landing right on top of a game controller. It was pretty funny. Then Ada entered from the other side, picked up the pieces, popped them together, and said, "I fixed it!" There was a lot less fixing than there had been in the first video, but the viewer could still see the inside of the controller. Through Nina's video magic, it looked like Ada had repaired it completely. The video seemed solid. In some ways it was their best. Then Ada scrolled through the comments to see how people reacted to it.

Most of the comments were positive:

Milton breaks it again!

Sick!

So this is what's inside my controller!

Unfortunately, there were a few not-so-nice ones:

Good stuff happens before 2:24

Can't that girl smile more?

:10 Yay! It's Milton. 2:24 zzzzzzz

It's not that Ada had never read the video comments before, but she hadn't read them in a while. Was she really so boring to watch? Why hadn't she noticed it herself? She watched the video again from the beginning. Milton really was funny. She replayed it again.

Maybe it was the sound of her voice? It was a

little nasal. Why had she picked that outfit?

She replayed it again.

Why wasn't she smiling? Was she in a bad mood the day they filmed it?

And again.

Should she wear lip gloss? Try a different hairstyle? A makeover? A paper bag? Ada closed the video and her laptop.

They all got together a little early on Saturday to come up with some ideas for how to keep people watching. It almost seemed like Milton and Nina had talked about it already. And it was clear that they'd both read the comments too, although neither mentioned it at first. Instead, Nina pulled up the metrics. She pointed out how the number of first-time views had gone down, as well as the number of times viewers had watched the whole video. Ada hated that everyone knew their audience didn't like her and no one was saying it out loud. They were just talking about a bunch of numbers that added up to her being boring. She wanted to get back to their original idea. Their videos had evolved to Milton just being goofy and breaking stuff. At this point, all the technical stuff had been taken out. It was like Ada didn't even need to be there.

"We reached our goal. We covered all the school supplies this year. So can't we go back to what we were doing in the beginning? When it was fun for all of us?" said Ada. "Does it really matter if we don't get any more subscribers?"

"Ada." Nina put a hand on Ada's shoulder. "Do you know what we could have here? It's so much more than a charity now. In a few months *we* could start making money off our views!"

"But not if people lose interest," said Milton. "Then you can forget it. We might as well not even bother."

"Well, I wouldn't want to ruin your shot at stardom, Milton," said Ada.

"Great, so stop being such a snooze fest," said Milton.

"Milton," said Nina, "Ada is not boring."

"Oh, I know she's not," said Milton. "But our viewers think so."

"Finally!" said Ada. "Someone says it out loud!"

Ada walked toward the door.

"Where are you going?" said Nina.

"You guys can do this one without me," said Ada. "I'm going to go home and do something exciting, like arrange my sock drawer!"

Chapter Five

PHASED OUT

Ada was sitting at her desk fiddling with a card her grandma sent her a few weeks ago for her birthday. It was pink and had a big fat flower on the front. Flowers often made Ada yawn, but this one was so plump and sweet looking. It was scented with rosewater. The front of the card said *Roses Are Red, Peonies Are Pink*. Inside

it said, *I sent you this card so your birthday won't stink!* Grandma Gert had written in big, loopy cursive, *Love you, sweetie! Don't these flowers remind you of birthday cake?* There was a ten-dollar bill inside.

Ada asked her mom, "Why don't people write like this anymore?"

Her mom said, "I'm not sure. I think maybe because people use keyboards all the time now. So they phased it out."

As she was thinking how she'd spend the ten dollars, a notification popped up on her computer. Ada got a sinking feeling when she saw the latest *Oh No!* video appear. It was the first one Nina and Milton had shot without her.

As Ada looked at Milton's goofy face in the thumbnail, that phrase, "phased out," came to mind. Ada had been phased out. She was no longer a useful part of what had been her own idea. She didn't think she would feel bad about it, but she did. Each new video was further away from Ada's original idea for the channel. Now it was all just a bunch of camera tricks and silly slapstick routines. If the channel were someone else's and Ada had seen it, she might have thought it was funny. But she wasn't having fun anymore. There were certainly better things she could be doing with her time. She just had to remember what those things were.

Nina messaged her:

Hey, did you see the new video? It's not the same without you.

Yeah, thought Ada, *it's less boring.* Ada was thinking about how to reply to Nina when a message popped up from Tycho.

Hey, are you around? I'm at Uncle Arnold's

house and I have something cool to show you.

Really? Now? I'm intrigued!

Yeah, you want to hang out?

!! Of course!

Ada walked over to Mr. Peebles's stoop. Tycho was there waiting for her with a busted old tablet. She sat down next to him.

"I'm surprised you're available. I thought you would be chasing SeeMe stardom," said Tycho.

Ada felt a little knot growing in her chest.

She kicked at a rock on the step below her and avoided Tycho's eyes. She didn't want to get all sad in front of him.

"Not doing that anymore."

"Yeah, I wondered why you weren't in the last one."

"It turns out I'm not the star. Of my *own* videos."

"They fired you?"

"Not exactly," said Ada. "But did you read the comments? Turns out I'm boring."

"Ada! You couldn't be boring if you tried. I always liked your part of the videos the best," said Tycho. "I was a little sad when they got shorter."

"You're just being nice!"

"No, really. There are lots of channels dedicated to breaking things. I like seeing stuff get better," said Tycho.

Tycho was good at cheering her up. He helped Ada see things in a different light.

"Speaking of making things better, what do you say we spruce up this tablet I found?" said Tycho.

Ada smiled and rubbed her hands together. The tablet Tycho showed Ada looked bad. The screen was all spiderwebbed with cracks and there were even pieces of glass missing. It could have been overwhelming. A lost cause. Utterly hopeless. But Ada felt far from hopeless. For the first time in a long time—well, since before she started *Oh No! I Broke It!*—Ada actually felt excited.

"Are we going to video it?" asked Ada.

"I mean, it's still a good idea," said Tycho. "But I understand you might be sick of video."

"Nah," said Ada. "Maybe we can learn something from it later."

Ada set up the camera on her makeshift stand, making sure to focus on the table and not to feature Tycho's face in the frame. Tycho pried away the screen of the tablet gently. There was dust all inside, so Ada swept it away with a small, soft-bristled brush. Then they checked

the connections, the home button, all the little wires and chips. The cool thing about the tablet was that it would look like a wreck at first. She could see why the person who had owned it left it in their trash bin. But underneath, almost everything about it was still good. It's like the tablet was smiling on the inside, but not on the outside. Ada concluded that it mostly just needed a good cleaning and a fresh piece of glass. After they pulled the whole thing apart and cleaned it up, they decided to take a bus with Mr. Peebles to Running in Circuits to get supplies.

Ada and Mr. Peebles waited on the sidewalk while the lift pulled Tycho inside the bus. Then they walked up the steps and took their seats next to him. Ada videoed the bus ride there and back to Juniper Garden. It was fun going places in the neighborhood with Mr. Peebles because he knew what everything used to be and how things had changed. Like Tycho, though, he was camera-shy, so Ada just captured the passing scenery while she recorded Mr. Peebles's voice.

"See that luxury apartment building over there?" he said. "It used to be a library when I was a kid. Beautiful old building."

It was a beautiful building. There was a flower motif along the tops of the columns. Ada had heard her mother call the columns "Corinthian," which sounded as fancy as it looked.

On the way back, they picked up Ada's favorite sesame noodles near Running in Circuits and ate them by Mr. Peebles's stoop as they finished their work. A group of Girl Scouts walked door-to-door selling cookies. When they got to Mr. Peebles's door, they stopped but didn't say anything for a minute. They were giggling and seemed shy.

"Hi there," said Ada.

The girls gently pushed the oldest one in the group toward Ada.

"Ahem, hi! Sorry, we were, um . . . We were just wondering if you were the girl in those SeeMe videos. The girl who fixes things?" she said.

"Oh!" Ada said, caught off guard. "Yes, that's me."

"We love your videos!" one of the smaller girls said. "We earned our Engineering badge by fixing our Tamagotchis thanks to your video." She held out her sash to show Ada the badge.

"Wow!" said Ada. "Congratulations!"

"Well, we just wanted to thank you," the older girl said. "It's not every day we see kids like us doing technical stuff."

"You're my hero!" the littlest Girl Scout squealed.

"Thank YOU!" said Ada. "Make sure you stop

at that door over there. My dad is addicted to
Thin Mints."

"We will!" said the little girl.

Ada watched them walk across the courtyard and knock on her door. Suddenly the comments about her being boring didn't mean so much anymore.

"That was pretty cool," Tycho said.

"Can't disagree with that," said Ada, smiling to herself.

Tycho and Ada put the final touches on the tablet. Even though Ada had been working with Tycho for the whole project, she couldn't believe her eyes when it was finished.

"Not bad, right?" said Tycho.

"It looks like it just came out of the box," said Ada.

"Needs one last touch," said Mr. Peebles.

He went upstairs and came down with a little tool called a Dremel. On the back of the tablet he etched A&T in perfect block print.

"There," he said. "Now it's a work of art."

Ada turned it on and started a game of chess with Tycho.

"You do your homework on a tablet?" Tycho asked.

"Sometimes. Sometimes I do it on my laptop," said Ada.

"Same. A lot of people don't have either, though."

"Yeah . . . And it seems like other people are just throwing them away. . . ." Ada trailed off, an idea forming in her mind.

When Ada got home, her dad was at the dining table finishing up a lesson plan.

"Hiya!" said Ada. She planted a big kiss on the top of his head.

"Well, my goodness!" said Mr. Lace. "What did I do to deserve that?"

"Just the usual spectacular dad stuff," said Ada.

"Well, I'm glad. And I'm glad to see you in such a good mood," said Mr. Lace.

"Yeah, you were totally right about the videos. I've never been so satisfied by quitting something! Now on to the next big project!"

Chapter Six

Hopeful Tablets

The next Tuesday, after school, Ada walked home with Crystal and Tanya. Ada's neighbor Jacob called to her from across the courtyard.

"Hey, Ada! Mr. Peebles told me you were looking for tablets," he said. He was holding three of them in his hands. "I keep meaning to recycle

these at Running in Circuits, but, you know, with the wedding prep and everything, Jeanie and I have been pretty busy."

"Oh, great!" said Ada.

"Jeanie has one with a big crack across it, but I don't suppose you want that," said Jacob.

"Oh, I do! I want it. We'll take any tablet, no matter how hopeless," said Ada.

"Ha! That's good! Is that your slogan?"

"Well, I guess it could be," said Ada.

Ada ran upstairs and sat at her desk. She had a new message. It was from Nina, who was at her aunt's house.

Are you working on social studies? Want to work on it together?

The year before, Nina and Ada would call each other on Speak-A-Boo all the time and just leave it on while they worked on homework and chatted about stuff. But in the two weeks since

Ada had stopped making videos, they still hadn't gotten back in their old groove. Ada didn't feel hurt about the videos anymore. They weren't much fun for her anyway. On the other hand, she was having lots of fun with the tablet project, but she missed her friend.

I can't right now. Chat later?

Kk

Ada charged each of the tablets for ten minutes, then turned them on. She wiped all

Jacob's information from them. One of them ran out of battery within five minutes. She made a note to replace the battery. Ada and Tycho had started a shared spreadsheet to keep track of their inventory. They numbered each tablet and made notes about things that needed fixing. Ada changed the title of the spreadsheet from "Tablets" to "Hopeful Tablets." She thought it was the perfect name for their project.

Tanya and Elliott hopped down the hallway as Ada worked. Elliott had developed his own form of tag where you couldn't use your hands and you had to tag with your foot. Tanya hopped through the door and landed in the doorway with a crash.

"Thanks for dropping in, Tanya," said Ada without looking up.

Tanya giggled. Then she stood and made her way over to Ada's desk.

"What are you doing with those? Elliott says you're fixing them," said Tanya.

"We're going to try. If we can't, we can use them for parts to fix other tablets," said Ada.

"Then you're gonna sell them?" Tanya asked.

"Nope. We're going to put them up for adoption," said Ada.

"You mean give them away? Like the one Elliott gave me?"

"Yeah. Do you know someone else who needs one?" Ada asked.

"My friend Grace has been sharing with me," said Tanya. "And my other friends Jamie and John share one. Sometimes Katya borrows mine. . . ."

Ada messaged Tycho.

Hey, we're going to need a lot more tablets.

As it turned out, almost no one in Tanya's class had a tablet of their own—they all shared about five. And yet they all needed them to access schoolwork. There were tablets that they could borrow from school, but sometimes there weren't enough for everyone. Even the tablets that were available were often slow or had other problems. And of course, there were many other classrooms in her school, all of which had a similar shortage of tablets. And there were more schools like Tanya's in the city. Even Ada's school, which was in a more affluent community, had students who didn't have their own computer or tablet.

Ada wiped down a tablet with an alcohol wipe and handed it to Tycho. Tycho looked the tablet over, made a note in the spreadsheet, and placed it in the box. Ada handed him another one. It had a big crack across the glass.

"This one's actually pretty new, but I guess it doesn't turn on anymore," said Ada. "The owner said he'd already replaced it because it was so expensive to fix, he might as well buy a new one."

Ada looked at the growing list of kids who needed tablets and tried not to get overwhelmed.

If they could help even a small fraction of the kids on that list, it would be worth it. So, for now, the focus was finding tablets and fixing them as quickly as they could so they could hand them over to students who needed them. Tanya helped with that last part by spreading the word to her friends. Tycho and Ada started to build a website, too, but they were slow in getting traffic to it.

Ada picked up another tablet. She heard a pinging noise and flipped it over to look at the screen. She realized the sound was coming from her pocket. It was a message from Nina.

Hey, it's been a while. Are we ever going to hang out again?

Ada felt a pang of guilt. She had missed a few messages from Nina recently because she had been so busy with the tablet project. The last few weeks had her so busy that she had hardly spent time with Nina at all. She'd only seen her at school. Sometimes she even spent lunchtime working on the tablet project. Some of the teachers had been collecting old ones for her.

Let's go get smoothies tomorrow, Ada typed back.

Okay!

Come to my house first. I want to show you something.

Chapter Seven

MAKING STUFF WITH FRIENDS

Holy mac 'n' cheese," said Nina. "People were throwing these away?"

"Or recycling them, yeah," said Ada.

She showed Nina the spreadsheets she'd made. One was for the tablets, and another was a waiting list of kids looking for tablets.

"As you can see, there are fewer finished tablets than there are people who need them," said Ada.

"Yeah. Geez," said Nina.

"We launched a website looking for volunteers and donations," said Ada, "but we need to get traffic to it."

"You should come on *Oh No!* again," said Nina.

"Oh, uh, no," said Ada.

"Yeah, I figured that's what you'd say," said Nina, "but you know, our traffic has been going down. It seems like maybe people are getting tired of seeing stuff get broken. Who knows, maybe this will be good for all of us!"

• • •

Ada had hoped Tycho would come with her to shoot the video, but he opted out.

You're better at this stuff than I am, Ada, he messaged. *gl!*

When Ada walked into Nina's room, Milton was reviewing the last video on Nina's computer.

"Hey, Milton," said Ada.

"Hey, Lace," said Milton. "Did you come to gloat?"

"Hmmm," said Ada. "I hadn't thought about that, but it's not a bad idea."

"You're funny, Ada," Milton said with a smile. "Now, if only we could capture that sense of humor on camera," said Milton. "You might save our careers!"

"Milton," said Nina. "We don't have careers. We're ten."

"How about you help me fix these tablets," Ada said, "and we'll go from there?"

Milton looked back at Ada and put his fingers to his chin. "Hmm. That could work. It might be fun to be, like, smart again. Instead of just going for laughs!"

"Yeah, I've missed that side of you," said Ada.

Ada pulled out the broken tablets she'd brought. She set one on the ground and walked back to the table to get in camera-ready position.

As Nina called "Action!," Milton walked into the frame and onto the tablet. He turned to the camera, shrugged, and sighed. "Not again . . ."

"We can fix that!" said Ada. For the first time in probably his whole life, Milton looked bashful.

In the second half of the video, Ada showed Milton how to open up a tablet. Together they talked about what was inside. Milton knew what a lot of the parts were already. He started on the second tablet by himself.

"Let me know if you need help with that screw," said Ada.

"Not a chance," said Milton. "For once I'm going to fix something!"

As they worked, Milton asked Ada about Hopeful Tablets. Ada told him about how she loved to fix stuff and how she and Tycho got the idea. She told him how the program worked and how many kids had tablets already, and that anyone could bring their tablet to the local library and connect to the internet there for free.

"Done!" Milton said, holding his repaired tablet up. "So I get to keep this now that I fixed it, right?"

"Sorry, Milton! All our tablets go to kids who need them." Ada then looked directly at the camera, feeling brave. "And if you're one of those kids, just sign up on our website!"

". . . which you can find in the description below!" said Milton. They both pointed down with their screwdrivers.

Nina cut the video and Ada started to laugh.

"That was fun! I've missed working with you guys!" she said.

"Yeah, it definitely hasn't been the same," said Milton. "Sorry how that all went down, Ada. I think the fame gave me a big head."

"You? No . . . ," Ada teased. "I'm just happy to be hanging with you two again."

They looked through the footage and talked about how to put together the final video. This was the first episode that Milton and Ada were really just playing themselves, and Ada felt more comfortable than she'd felt in their previous videos.

Despite her nervousness, Ada had actually enjoyed filming this episode of *Oh No!* Her first thought was that maybe if she and Milton had had more fun together like this in other videos, people would have liked watching them more. Then she realized that not thinking about people liking them was partially why they enjoyed making the video.

Ada turned to Nina. "This is gold, Nina. Thank you!"

"I'm so glad you like it!" Nina said proudly.

It felt good to be making stuff with friends.

They posted the new *Oh No!* video a few days later. It was the most popular one yet. A lot of people interested in Hopeful Tablets watched and shared it and there was "mad traffic," Milton said. From that video and ongoing traffic from their older videos, they earned a whopping additional ten thousand dollars.

Nina, Milton, and Ada met up in Juniper Garden after school to discuss their next steps.

"That video was pure fire!" Nina said.

"Yeah, looks like we're back!" said Milton. "What do you want to do next?"

"It was really fun," Ada said. "And maybe we can do another one at some point, but Hopeful Tablets keeps me plenty busy."

"All right, Ada," said Milton. "You don't have to beg! We'll help you."

"You read me like a book, Milton," said Ada. "I'm glad you're into it, because I was thinking we could give the money to the library? Tanya said it was really busy when she was there. I bet they could use more supplies."

"Huh," Milton said. "That's a nice thought. . . . Not as much fun as a pizza party, though."

"Why not both?" Nina said. "Let's celebrate with the whole town!"

It took some work to turn the library grounds into a fairground. Ada arrived at the library early with Nina and Milton to set up the tablet swap area and help assemble booths. There were games,

music, and food. Nina opened a face-painting booth, and Milton set up a racecourse with some of his remote control cars. Tablet donors and receivers got ten free tickets for the amusements.

Crystal brought Tanya and a bunch of Tanya's classmates. Elliott and Tanya didn't move from the Skee-Ball table, unless it was to go throw darts at balloons. They were fierce competitors. Tycho's mom brought a whole bunch of homemade donuts to sell. Tycho told Ada he'd been smelling them for the past two days.

"It's a miracle that they all made it here," said Ada.

"I had to test a few," said Tycho. "And then a few more. Let's just say that I might have eaten into the profits a little."

Tycho, Ada, and Mr. Peebles set up the tablets and customized them. All of them were hand-engraved by Mr. Peebles with their new company name, Hopeful Tablets. Mr. Peebles had been super helpful. He even brought in a couple of his friends to help with the repairs. When Ada checked their stats before the end of the day, they had given away almost a hundred tablets. They had also added another hundred names to the waiting list of students who needed tablets. But every one of Tanya's classmates got one.

The game that Ada had looked forward to most, though, was the tank where you could dunk Mr. Lace. She'd watched her classmates throw softballs at the target all day long, but she had been too busy to take a turn. Right before four o'clock both Nina and Milton made their way over to the dunking booth line, just as Mr. Lace dried off for the fiftieth time. Ada couldn't stand by and watch her friends dunk her dad. As Milton was picking up the ball, Ada ran over.

"Hold on there, Miltie," said Ada. "I think I've got dibs."

"Fair enough," said Milton. He handed Ada the ball. She stood sideways and took aim at the target.

"Ada, put the ball down," said Mr. Lace.

"Or . . . ?" asked Ada.

"You're grounded?" said Mr. Lace. He didn't seem sure about his answer.

"You would ground me when I provide a valuable service to the community?" said Ada.

"Ada," said Ms. Lace. "Take pity on your pop."

"Really?" said Ada. Ms. Lace held out her hand. She had a look that showed she meant business.

"Okaaaaay," said Ada. She dropped the ball into her mother's palm.

"Thanks, hon," said Mr. Lace. He looked relieved.

Ms. Lace wound up and threw the ball straight at the bull's-eye. The platform beneath Mr. Lace gave way and he plunged into the tank full of water below. Nina and Milton doubled over in laughter. Mr. Lace pulled himself out of the tank.

"Poor Dad," said Elliott.

"Thank you, Elliott," said Mr. Lace. "At least I have one loyal family member."

"I'm sorry, honey. It just happened!" said Ms. Lace.

"You could have just taken tickets at one of the other game booths," said Ada.

Mr. Lace coughed up some more water. Ada handed him a towel.

"I thought this would be more fun," said Mr. Lace.

"It was!" said Ms. Lace. "Just maybe not for you."

"Are you kidding?" said Mr. Lace. "What could be more fun than seeing my kids do amazing things?"

"Agreed," said Ms. Lace. "How many tablets did you give away today, Ada?"

"One hundred!" said Ada.

"Not bad for a day's work," said Ms. Lace.

"And it's just the beginning!" said Ada.

Behind the Science

E-Bikes

An electric bike, or an "e-bike" for short, is simply a bike with an electric motor attached that helps make pedaling a little easier. These motors are powered by rechargeable batteries mounted on the bike. The benefit of a bike like this is that it makes it easier for bicyclists to take longer trips, to go up steep hills, and to carry heavier things with them. It can also make biking easier for riders who are older or have disabilities. Many e-bikes allow you to change the level of assistance the motor gives you, so you can either receive a gentle push or kick things into gear and feel a boost of power! More and more people are choosing to commute to school and work with e-bikes over traditional cars.

The Internet

The internet is a powerful tool. It can allow you to watch fun videos, do your homework, or even start your own company. It's a tool that can make your life more enjoyable and also easier, but not everyone has access to it. In fact, only half of the world is connected to the internet. Why is that? Well, usually the way that people get access to the internet is through a web of cables that physically connect their home, school, or library to the world wide web. And once that web of cables is created, you have to pay to use it! The reason some people aren't connected is either because they live far away from these cables, or they simply can't afford to use them. Today, there are companies who are trying to beam internet down from space using satellites to help better connect people who live out in remote areas. But this still costs money. Hopefully one day we will be able to connect every kid around the globe. Until then, it's great to support places that offer internet for free to the public, like libraries!

NICHROME WIRE

Electric hair dryers are pretty simple machines. They work by blowing air through a small contraption that gets really hot and then hot air comes out the other end. The cool part about a hairdryer is that small contraption that gets hot. It gets hot by circulating current through a special material: nichrome wire. Nichrome wire is unique because it's a special type of metal alloy that can get really hot by passing electrical current through it (an alloy is something that is a mix of metals or a metal with a non-metal). When you plug in your hairdryer and turn it on, you're passing electrical current through the nichrome wire, which makes it really hot. There is also nichrome wire in many electrical toasters. When you turn your toaster on, electrical current passes through the nichrome wire, making the inside of your toaster really hot. This makes your bread nice and toasty (just don't leave it in there too long or the bread will burn! Material science of metal alloys is fascinating and is used in many of the technologies we use every day—like toasters and hairdryers!

PROFESSIONAL LIGHTING

Nina helped Ada learn the value of good lighting when it came to filming. There is both an art and a science to professional lighting that people who work in film production get really good at! One special type of lighting used in video production is called "three point lighting." This involves a "key light," a "fill light," and a "backlight." The key light is the primary light and the brightest light source of the three. It's usually less bright and directed at your main subject (like Ada) at an angle. The "fill light" will usually be on the opposite side of the camera and helps fill in the shadows that the key light creates. The backlight shines on your subject from behind and helps separate them from the background in your shot.

LIBRARIES

Libraries are incredible community hubs that help support the creation of healthy communities. In addition to lending out books, libraries and librarians help lift up the most vulnerable members in your neighborhood. Through vital resources like the internet and a vast supply of books, librarians can help people learn about jobs in an area, research options for a place to live, or figure out what health services might be available to them. Libraries lift up and support many members of a community including children and their families, veterans, the elderly, and immigrants. My family loves to visit our local library for read-aloud and crafting activities. My kids love it! Reach out to your local library to learn about fun events and activities hosted there throughout the year!

Acknowledgments

Firstly, I want to acknowledge my co-author, Tamson, who has helped infuse so much heart and soul into every Ada Lace story. And Renée, your illustrations effortlessly capture the energy and emotion of every single scene. It is such a joy to work with the both of you. I also want to express my gratitude to my phenomenal agent, Jennifer Keene, whose tireless advocacy for my ideas has continually opened up new doors and opportunities. I also want to thank my manager, Kyell Thomas, for his guidance over the last eight years. The two of you have helped me steer this ship of mine into new, wonderful, and unexpected adventures. Thank you to my editor, Dainese Santos; your keen eye has been instrumental in crafting this story. And finally, my family—Tom, Rose, and Lincoln. Every bit of life is made more joyful simply because you exist to share it with. Thank you for being mine.